entors,
riosity and inspire
ience and inventions!

bhirami,
me to share my passion
pus to life. Thank you!

y on the way,
what lies ahead.

ion and a pile of junk.
n

D0814341

Pumpus loved to read about great ideas and inventions. His favorite inventors were Thomas Edison, Albert Einstein and Nikola Tesla.

Pumpus had two best friends, Filbin and Filberta, who loved to hang out with him, especially when he went on Halloween adventures.

It was a perfect autumn morning.
Pumpus and his friends
were planning for a long hike
up the nearby mountains
to camp overnight.

After they set up the tent, the friends collected wood, bark, and dry grass to make a campfire.

Pumpus suddenly realized ....

...he had forgotten the matches to light the wood.

"Oh, no!" said Filberta and Filbin, and they wondered if the fun they had planned for Halloween might turn out to be a disappointment.

Luckily, Pumpus had brought his book of inventions, where he kept the best ideas of his favorite inventors.

"*Boon-dah!*" Pumpus yelled. "I have an idea. Let's MAKE fire."

"How can you make fire?" asked the surprised Filbin.

"Don't you need matches?" asked Filberta.

"It says here that fire is made by friction," explained Pumpus. "And friction is what happens when things like the palms of your hands rub together. Friction also produces heat."

Filberta and Filbin grew very excited.

Pumpus took his blade and sharpened the tip of a small Aspen stick being careful to follow the rules he learned in safety training school.

He put the tip in a hole inside a large piece of Aspen wood and rubbed quickly.

Nothing happened. "Uh-Oh!" said Filberta and Filbin who worried they wouldn't be able to see in the dark after sunset.

But then, something happened.

A wisp of smoke rose from the wood. Then, a glowing hot coal formed. "The glowing hot coal is called an ember," Pumpus explained. "And that's how a fire begins."

Pumpus gently placed the ember in the center of the dry grass they had rolled into a ball.

Pumpus made fire! "Hooray!" said Filberta and Filbin in amazement, and they gave Pumpus a big hug!

That night, the three friends carved pumpkins, lit their Jack-o-lanterns, and best of all...

took turns telling ghost stories while toasting marshmallows.

And it was the best Halloween ever!

PUMPUSVILLE TIMES

Vol. 1   Pumpus, Chief Editor   www.boon-dah.com

Topic of the Day – FIRE

The invention of fire and its uses was very important to early humans for many reasons.

<u>Protection</u> – Campfire gave them protection from wild animals and kept them warm in colder climates. Being able to start a campfire at any place they wanted, gave early humans the ability to camp in better locations.

<u>Cooking</u> – Making their own fires let early humans cook their food. Cooked food did not carry disease-causing germs and was easier to digest than raw food. Cooked food also provided them with more energy to stay healthy and fit.

<u>Socializing</u> – Once early humans used fire to cook their food, they sat together around their fire in larger groups to socialize. This encouraged people to invent a language so they could talk to each other and exchange stories. Sitting around fire in larger groups also made them feel safer and more secure.

<u>Light</u> – Fire provided light in the night so they could see each other in the dark since light bulbs hadn't been invented yet. They could also work or travel during the night since it could help them see where they were going.

What Do You Think?

Can you think of other reasons how the invention of fire changed the way humans lived back then? How about today?
Have you ever had a campfire? What kinds of things did you do around the campfire? Are they similar to what early humans did?

Want to Learn More?
Here are Some Ideas to Check Out:

Book – "Ideas: A History of Thought and Invention, from Fire to Freud" by Peter Watson (2006, Harper Perennial)

Book – "Catching Fire: How Cooking Made Us Human" by Richard Wrangham (2010, Basic Books)

Safety Topic of the Day – FIRE SAFETY

Fire is very dangerous and can easily burn you. Even a little candle on a birthday cake can cause a severe burn or fire. Here are some safety tips for when you are around fire.

<u>Matches & Lighters</u> – Never play with matches or lighters. These are not toys and can easily burn you. If you find matches or a lighter, stop what you are doing and take them to an adult right away so they can be put away in a safe place.

<u>Cooking</u> – Never touch an oven, stovetop, or pan used for cooking. Ovens, stovetops, and pans do not always look hot, and there is not always someone near them when they are. Just reaching for the handle of a pan may cause it to fall over and spill on you and burn your face or skin. Be safe and just don't touch them. Always ask an adult for help cooking and for permission to touch anything that may be hot, such as a pan sitting on the counter or a table.

<u>Campfires</u> – Never light a campfire. Campfires are fun, but they are very dangerous, and should only be lit by an adult. Always stay at least 3 feet away from any burning fire and don't pick up things that have been sitting in the fire. If something falls into the fire, ask an adult for help right away. Never leave a campfire unattended and make sure the fire is completely out when you are done or leave the campsite.

Practice Your Safety Skills!

What would you do if your clothes caught on fire? If this were to happen, just remember these three, simple words: STOP, DROP, and ROLL. This is what they mean:

STOP – Stop whatever you're doing and stop screaming, crying, and panicking.
DROP – Drop to the ground or floor immediately.
ROLL – Roll over and over to try and put out all the flames.

It's important to practice these steps so you will do them automatically.

To Learn More on Fire Safety, Check Out These Websites:

http://www.usfa.fema.gov/prevention....
http://www.firesafekids.org
http://safekids.org

Another Fine Edit by www.awriterforlife.com

Made in the USA
Middletown, DE
22 February 2019